39 Ways to Open Your Heart

39 WAYS TO OPEN YOUR HEART

An Illuminated Meditation

Arlene Gay Levine

Illustrated by Karen Kroll

CONARI PRESS

Conari Press books are distributed by Publishers Group West.

ISBN: 0–943233–90–9

COVER DESIGN: Ame Beanland and Judy July
COVER ILLUSTRATION: Karen Kroll
CALLIGRAPHY: Magué Calanché
BOOK DESIGN & LAYOUT: Ame Beanland and Judy July

Library of Congress Cataloging-in-Publication Data
Levine, Arlene Gay 1949-
    39 ways to open your heart/written by Arlene Gay Levine: illustrated by Karen Kroll.
    p. cm.
ISBN 0-943233-90-9 (hardcover)
    1. Self-help techniques.   I. Title.
BF632.L483   1996
158'.1—dc20   95-25519

PRINTED IN HONG KONG
10 9 8 7 6 5 4 3 2 1

from Arlene

*F*or Alan and Lenny, my two original ways.

from Karen

I *B*elieve in the ability to transcend One's outer shell,
     One's inner thought, One's plane of existence
   *L*ove is the constant wave
        rolling over individual intellects
        gathering us up
             —inviting us to be whole
   *U*nderstand as me, as you, as <u>we</u>
        Life is a state of mind.

Acknowledgments

*I*t is with pleasure that I acknowledge the publishers of
Conari Press, Mary Jane Ryan and Will Glennon, who
believed in my vision from the start. I am deeply grateful
for their enthusiasm, wisdom, and guidance.

I add very special thanks to Mary Jane for her insightful
editorial suggestions. Heartfelt gratitude goes to Karen Kroll
for her miraculous artwork. My sincere appreciation to
Karen Bouris for her commitment to this project.

39 Ways to Open Your Heart

*P*lanted deep in the heart of each of us is an urge to grow that carries us forward from one level of life to the next. Like the buds of early spring, we are called to unfold in a spiral evolutionary dance. Yet sometimes this impulse to become all we can be gets bogged down in the weeds of daily living.

What do you do when you are tired of battling with the difficult moments of daily life? Have a drink? Eat too much? Get depressed? So many of our solutions only sink us deeper into despair. When times are tough, we can learn to make room in our hearts for ourselves, choosing to connect with the healing energy within us all. Opening our hearts to ourselves, to those around us, and to life itself is a way of softening toward all that is difficult, easing the way with the balm of compassion.

You have the ability to open your heart at any moment. Reacquaint yourself with the geography of your own restorative powers by meditating on the sayings and illustrations in this little book. Read it from front to back or open it at random for self-guided inspiration on your interior journey back to joy. In times of need, one of the *39 Ways to Open Your Heart* may suddenly arise in your mind, the painting floating gently into view.

Whether given as a gift to yourself, a friend, or a loved one, *39 Ways to Open Your Heart* is a gesture of support and care. I hope it helps guide you to the fertile territory of your open heart.

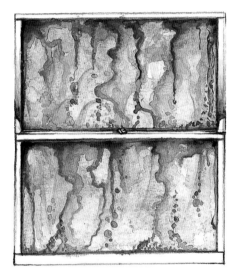

Let it cry.

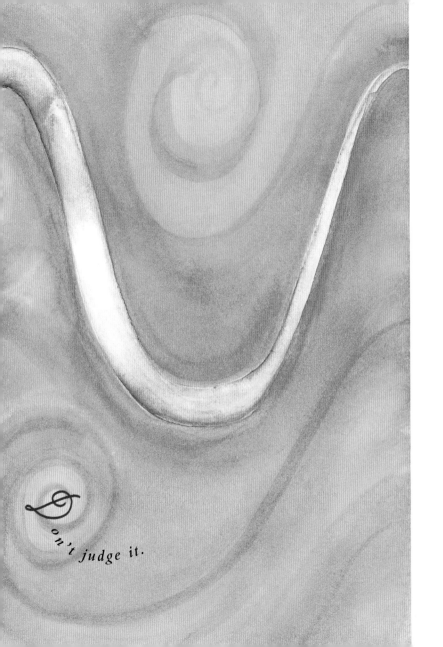

*D*on't judge it.

Give it space.

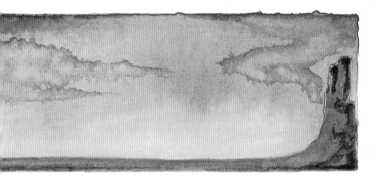

$\mathcal{L}$*et it struggle.*

Place no expectations on it.

Ask it what it needs.

Spend silent time with it.

Remove the filter of fear from its eyes.

Help it mourn past injustices and release them.

Guide it to see choices.

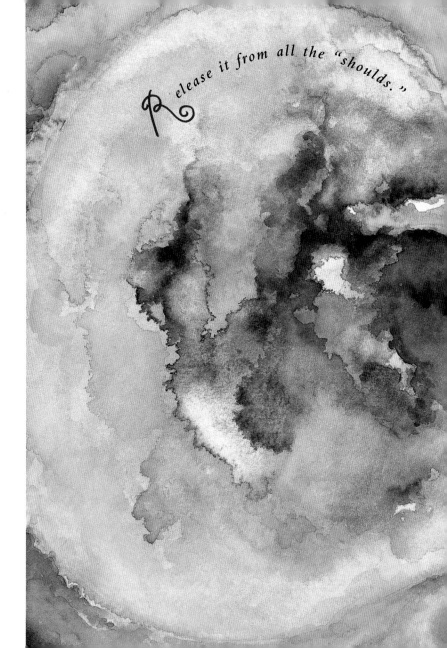

Release it from all the "shoulds."

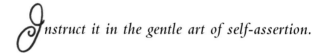

Instruct it in the gentle art of self-assertion.

Teach it the art of waiting.

Sing to it.

Make today into an adventure for it.

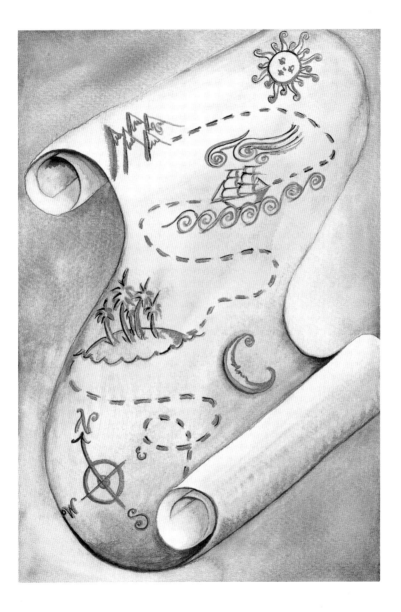

Allow it to question everything.

*W*elcome all its feelings.

Support its decisions.

Treasure the innocent child in it.

*Q*uiet its critical voices.

ring balance into its life.

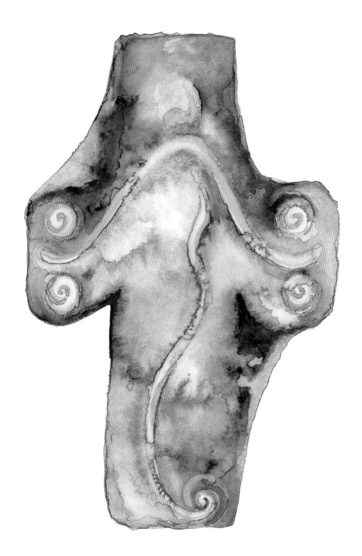

Tell it jokes.

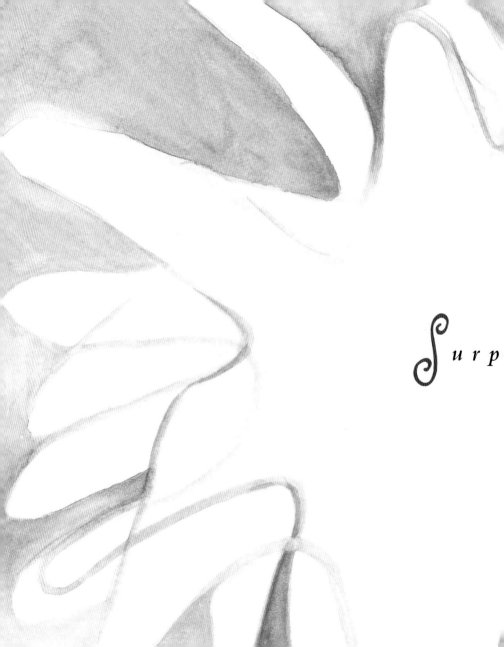

$\int u\, r\, p$

e it!

Surround it with fresh flowers.

Give it permission to be less than perfect.

Learn the lessons it has to teach.

Surrender to the moment with it.

Cherish its eccentricities.

Challenge it to climb to the source of a waterfall.

Remind it of the transformative power of gratitude.

*W*rite a poem to it.

Admire its unique abilities.

*M*ake a wish come true for it.

Take it for a moonlit walk through freshly fallen snow.

Praise it for attempts as

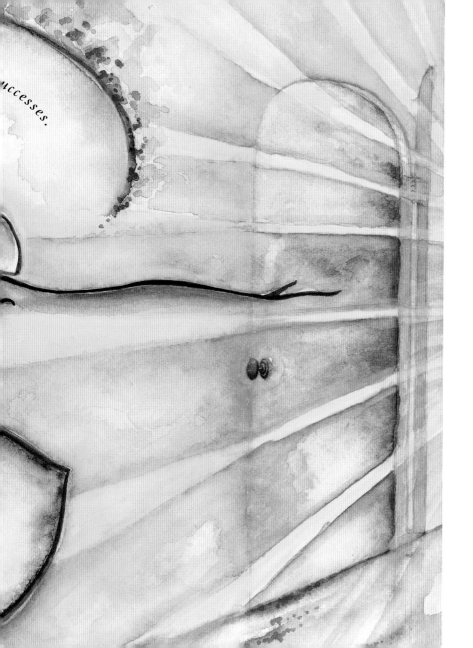

successes.

Allow it to change its mind.

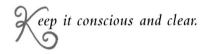

Keep it conscious and clear.

Forgive it.

Let it be the star in the movie of its life.

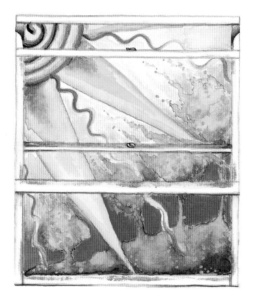

About the Authors

*A*rlene Gay Levine has been an educator for over two decades. She is the creator of Logo Therapy™ seminars where she "teaches people how to use words to change their lives closer to their hearts' desires." Her writing has appeared in the *New York Times*, literary journals, and anthologies. She lives in New York City where she is currently at work on her poetry and a new screenplay.

*K*aren Kroll is an artist who lives on the island of Maui.

Conari Press, established in 1987, publishes books on topics ranging from spirituality and inspiration, to sexuality and personal growth. Our main goal is to publish quality books that will make a difference in people's lives—both how we feel about ourselves and how we relate to one another.

Our readers are our most important resource, and we value your input, suggestions, and ideas. We'd love to hear from you—after all we are publishing books for you!

For a complete catalog or to get on our mailing list, please contact us at:

CONARI PRESS

2550 Ninth Street, Suite 101, Berkeley, CA 94710
800-685-9595 • fax: 510-649-7190 • e-mail: Conaripub@aol.com